MW01115136

Ryder Shava

Rosen
REAL
READERS

Rosen
Classroom™
New York

The sky is blue today.

The weather is warm.

There are no clouds in the sky.

It will not rain today.
We play outside.

We draw pictures with chalk.

We take turns jumping rope.

We have a picnic.
What a nice blue sky day!